FOX AND SQUIRREL

Ruth Ohi

Scholastic Canada Ltd.
Toronto New York London Auckland Sydney
Mexico City New Delhi Hong Kong Buenos Aires

Scholastic Canada Ltd.
604 King Street West, Toronto, Ontario M5V 1E1, Canada

Scholastic Inc.
557 Broadway, New York, NY 10012, USA

Scholastic Australia Pty Limited
PO Box 579, Gosford, NSW 2250, Australia

Scholastic New Zealand Limited
Private Bag 94407, Botany, Manukau 2163, New Zealand

Scholastic Children's Books
Euston House, 24 Eversholt Street, London NW1 1DB, UK

www.scholastic.ca

Library and Archives Canada Cataloguing in Publication
Ohi, Ruth
Fox and Squirrel / by Ruth Ohi.
ISBN 978-1-4431-1915-3
I. Title.
PS8579.H47F69 2013a   jC813'.6   C2013-901796-8

Author photo by Annie T.

6 5 4 3 2 1   Printed in Malaysia 108   13 14 15 16 17

For Kaarel — R.O.

"We are very different," said Squirrel.

"Not that different," said Fox.

4

"You're so big," said Squirrel.

"Not that big," said Fox.

"I like to climb," said Squirrel. "You can't."

"You climb well," said Fox.

Bzzzz

"I live in a nest," said Squirrel.

"You live in a burrow."

"Both are safe and warm," said Fox.

8

"I eat nuts and berries," said Squirrel.

"So do I," said Fox. "Sometimes."

"I like the day," said Squirrel,

"... and you like the night."

"We both like sunsets," said Fox.

"It's raining!" said Squirrel.

"It's raining!" said Fox.

Splash!

Sploosh!

"How can you two be friends?" said Rat.

"You are both so different!"

"Not so different," said Squirrel.

"We both have pointy ears,"
said Squirrel. "And bushy tails!"

"Well, bushy sometimes,"
said Fox.

drip

"We both like to run and play...

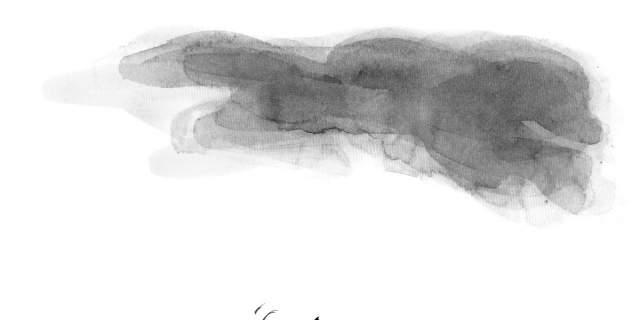

… and rest," said Squirrel.

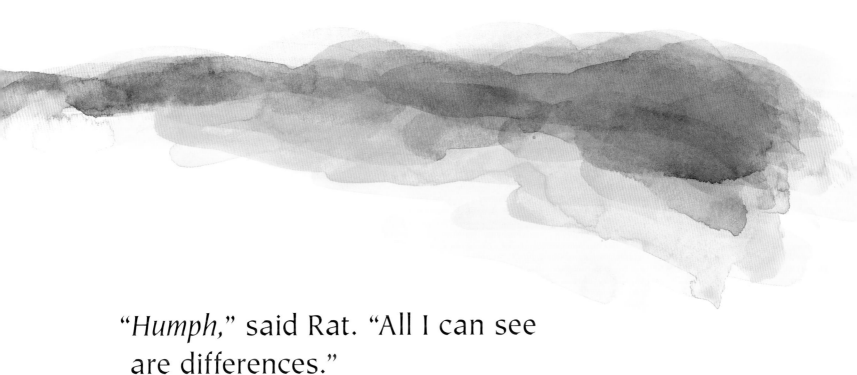

"*Humph,*" said Rat. "All I can see are differences."

And then Rat crawled back into his hole.

"We both get cold," said Squirrel.

Aa-choo

27

"We both like to be warm," said Fox.

"What are friends for?" said Squirrel.